BIG HERO 6
HIRO AND TADASHI

by **BRITTANY CANDAU**

illustrated by **JEFFREY CLARK**, **SCOTT TILLEY**, and **LORI TYMINSKI**

DISNEP PRESS

NEW YORK · LOS ANGELES

For MC
and DR—
the best
brother duo
around!
—B.C.

For Sam, Jillian,
and Carolyn
—J.C.

For my daughter,
Jennifer, the
most creative
person I know
—L.T.

To Momma
and DT
—S.T.

Designed by Tony Fejeran

Copyright © 2014 Disney Enterprises, Inc. All rights reserved. Published by Disney Press, an imprint of Disney Book Group. No part of this book may be reproduced or transmitted in any form or by any means, electronic or mechanical, including photocopying, recording, or by any information storage and retrieval system, without written permission from the publisher. For information, address Disney Press, 1101 Flower Street, Glendale, California 91201.

Printed in the United States of America

First Edition 10 9 8 7 6 5 4 3 2 1

ISBN 978-1-4847-0831-6   G942-9090-6-14220

Library of Congress Control Number: 2014935101

Visit www.disneybooks.com

Visit http://movies.disney.com/big-hero-6

That's me in that picture. The good-looking one. Okay, the small one. I'm Hiro Hamada. And that's my older brother, Tadashi. Back when we were younger. And this is the story of how we came up with the number one rule for being a Hamada brother.

It started like any other Monday. We'd spent most of the morning helping our aunt Cass at the café before school.

We were also thinking of new rules to add to our list. It's just the two of us, you see, so it's a pretty exclusive club.

We need to make sure we give us Hamada brothers a good name.

RULE 451:
HAMADA BROTHERS NEVER use something as LAME as a NOTEBOOK.

After Tadashi and I ran into our friend Fred, we came up with rules 453 and 454.

Then we reached San Fransokyo Tech, Tadashi's school and the top robotics college in the country. Even though I have a promising career in bot fighting, I REALLY want to go there next year.

Luckily, right after school, I got the **BEST NEWS EVER**. Tadashi convinced Professor Callaghan to let me work on the project, too.

So we met Tadashi's friends at one of our favorite places for inspiration: the junkyard.

Honey, Wasabi, and Go Go are also students at SF Tech. And Fred . . . well, he just likes hanging out.

Then Honey came up with a **GREAT** idea.

Let's surprise each other with our projects at the end of the week. Then we can decide which one really has the WOW factor!

Now we were talking.

A competition.

It was totally GAME ON!

I usually like to work alone. But my brother and I knew if we joined forces, we'd come up with something **BRILLIANT**.

So Tadashi and I hurried back to the café to come up with the greatest invention ever.

RuLe 456: HaMaDa bRotheRs' PRojects have to be CRAZY AWESOME!

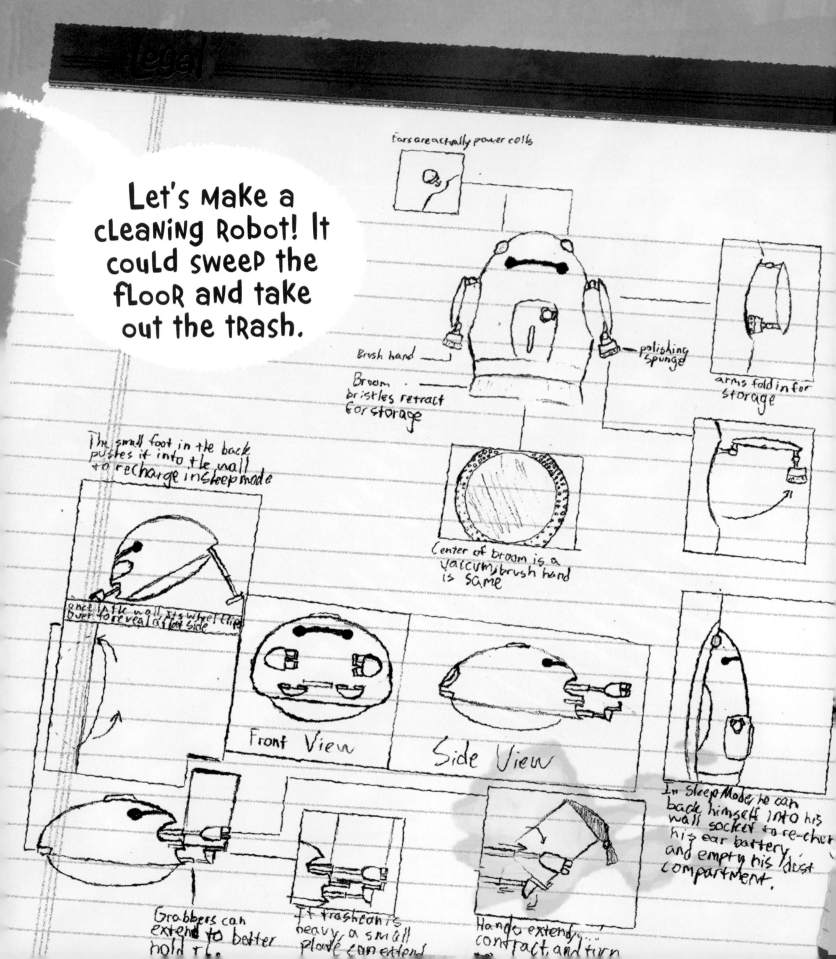

"It could light up fireplaces and candles and just be supercool!"

But for some reason, Tadashi wasn't into it.

"What about an energy-saving robot?" Tadashi asked.
"One that turns off all the things that aren't being used."

"Or a super-sushi-chef robot! One that feeds us and puts on a show at the same time!" I countered.

Finally, we shared our top-secret project. And boy, did it amaze them!

The world's first flying cat, complete with rocket boots!
We explained just how we'd gotten this genius idea.